DATE DUE		

FIC
ORT

3 66563 0902906 1
Ortega, Cristina.

The eyes of the
weaver = Los ojos
del tejedor

The Eyes Of The Weaver

THE EYES OF THE WEAVER

LOS OJOS DEL TEJEDOR

Cristina Ortega

Illustrated by Patricio E. García

University of New Mexico Press
Albuquerque

University of New Mexico Press edition published 2006

Printed and bound in China through Four Colour Imports, Ltd.

11 10 09 08 07 06   1 2 3 4 5 6

Library of Congress Cataloging-in-Publication Data

Ortega, Cristina, 1953–
    The eyes of the weaver : los ojos del tejedor / Cristina Ortega ; illustrated by Patricio E. García.
        p. cm.
    Summary: Ten-year-old Maria Cristina goes to visit her grandfather so that he can teach her to weave, as her family in northern New Mexico has done for seven generations.
    ISBN-13: 978-0-8263-3990-4 (cloth : alk. paper)
    ISBN-10: 0-8263-3990-5 (cloth : alk. paper)
  [1. Grandfathers—Fiction. 2. Weaving—Fiction. 3. New Mexico—Fiction. 4. Mexican Americans—Fiction.] I. Title: Ojos del tejedor. II. Garcia, Patricio, 1933– ill. III. Title.
    PZ7.O755Ey 2006
    [Fic]—dc22
                                    2005018103

Book composition by Damien Shay
Body type is Garamond 20/28
Display type is Bermuda LP Squiggle and Avant Garde

Juan Melquiades Ortega
1889 – 1992

Apolonia Martínez Ortega
1892 – 1967

This book is dedicated to my paternal grandparents.
The genius of my grandparents to share so much about their
lives through first-hand experiences and storytelling has
inspired me to write this true story.

Juan Melquiades Ortega was taught to weave by his father.
In those early days, weavers in the Chimayó Valley of northern
New Mexico sheared their own sheep. They spun and dyed
the wool for their blankets. At the age of fifteen my grandpa
began selling his own weavings.

He married Apolonia Martinez and together they raised eleven
children. They managed their small farm, and at the same time
kept up the tradition of weaving. My grandma helped her
husband choose color combinations for Chimayó blankets.

Life was hard in the valley. Like other farmers, my grandpa sold
his beautiful handwoven blankets to help support his family.
My grandma and her children kept up the farm and cared for
the animals when jobs took Juan far away into the mountains.

Juan Melquiades Ortega became well known as a master weaver.
He continued weaving until he was one hundred years old,
when his eyesight failed him.

Today some of his work and tools of the trade make up the
ten-year exhibit, "American Encounters," at the National Museum
of American History, Smithsonian Institution, in Washington, D.C.

Dad smiled as he walked away from the telephone and placed his hand on my shoulder. "It's all set, Cristina!" he said. "You can stay with your grandpa. He is ready to teach you how to weave."

Uh-oh. How could I stay by myself with Grandpa? I couldn't understand Spanish without other adults around. There wouldn't be anyone to translate his Spanish into English for me!

Mom saw the worried look on my face.

"Don't worry, *Jita*, this is the perfect time for you to learn how to weave. You can learn more Spanish, too!" she said.

"Your mother is right," Dad added. "This Ortega family has been making beautiful Chimayó weavings for seven generations. Just imagine, *imagínate*, since the time of your great, great, great, great, great grandfather! How do you feel about making it *eight* generations?"

"OK, I guess." What else could I say?

My grandpa's house in Chimayó was the place I loved best in all of New Mexico, and I loved to go there. But this time I was worried. Just this morning Mom told me it was my responsibility to make my bed. Now my parents were expecting me to become an eighth-generation weaver!

"Listen, Cristina," Mom said. "Why don't you call *Tía Elcia*? Ask if your cousin Annalisa can stay with you and Grandpa."

Calling Aunt Elsie was the best idea I'd heard yet!

My cousin Annalisa was a brain and she could speak Spanish!

My *tía* agreed to let Annalisa stay with Grandpa and me. She would meet us in Santa Fé and drive us to Grandpa's house in Chimayó.

In Santa Fé, Annalisa and I hugged and
squealed with delight. We felt so grown up to be
left alone with Grandpa! Dad said we'd better hurry
because Grandpa would be waiting for us girls.
At last we were on our way.

From the back seat I stared out at the rolling hills spotted with green juniper and behind them, the mighty Sangre de Cristo Mountains.

For miles we rode in silence.

Tía glanced at me through the rearview mirror and said, "Your grandpa is proud that you want to learn weaving."

"What if I can't learn to weave like Grandpa?"

"No one expects you to weave like Grandpa! He is a master weaver. He's been weaving since he was fifteen years old." *Tía* continued, "Cristina, all you have to do is listen and learn the best you can."

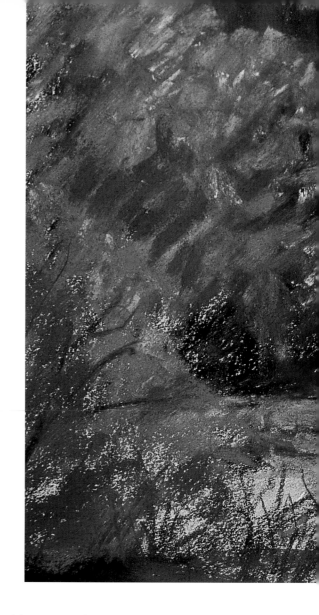

North of Santa Fé, *Tía* followed a narrow road that curved back and forth toward the mountains like a never-ending ribbon. Soon we could see the Chimayó Valley and the village where my family had lived for so many generations. And there was my grandpa's house.

Memories of family get-togethers, wagon rides,

hunting for chicken eggs, and evenings of staring into the starry sky filled my head.

This visit would be different.

This time I would learn how to weave Chimayó blankets. My love for Grandpa was bigger than the earth, but would we find a way to communicate, Juan Melquiades, *el tejedor*, and I?

As *Tía Elcia* parked the car alongside the house, Grandpa stepped out from the doorway. He gave us *una sonrisa*, a smile as warm as the sun.

I hurried to my grandpa *con un abrazo y un besito*. My hug and kiss always brought a loving twinkle to his eyes. Because I was his only redheaded grandchild, I enjoyed pretending his eyes twinkled especially for me, María Cristina, because he was a redhead too.

After we carried our bags inside I excused myself. I went up to the *casita*, the little house where my grandpa created beautiful Chimayó weavings with his old loom and colorful wools. I went inside the *casita* and closed the door.

I took a deep breath. The sweet fragrance of wool filled the dark, cool room. I went to Grandpa's big loom and gently strummed the many strands of scratchy white warp as though I were playing a

harp. I knew Grandpa's colorful Chimayó designs would soon be woven across the white strands of the warp.

No one knew about my special wish. I had always wanted to learn how to weave a Chimayó blanket. Now my wish was going to come true. But could I learn enough to be a real weaver like the other Ortegas? Could I carry on the family tradition?

Before *Tía Elcia* left, she gave us last-minute instructions. She reminded Annalisa and me that our grandpa was an early riser, so we should go to bed soon.

Tía told us to turn off the TV, *el mono*, when Grandpa asked us to. "*¿Entienden?* He doesn't like the television on late."

"We understand," Annalisa and I called out as she walked out to her car.

Grandpa, Annalisa, and I waved good-bye from the steps as the car disappeared down the narrow dirt road into the dust and darkness of the night.

That night in bed I was so nervous and excited! It took me a long time to go to sleep.

It felt as if I had just closed my eyes when I heard the distant crow of a rooster.

I felt someone nudge me. I opened my eyes.

"*Levántate,*" Grandpa whispered.

——Get up? Now? I wondered sleepily.

"*Tenemos mucho que hacer,*"

——what does he mean, "We have much to do?"

"*Ya está el almuerzo.*"

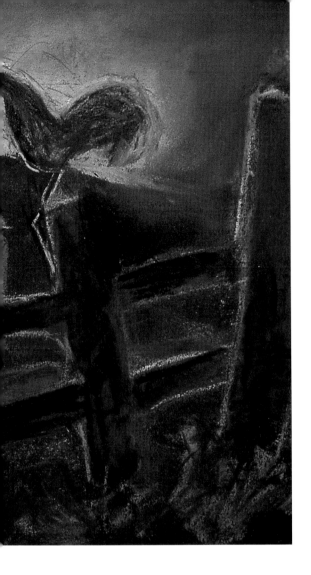

——Breakfast was ready. Mmm, I could smell his homemade *tortillas*.

I dragged myself out of bed. *Ay-yai-yai!* This was the earliest I'd ever gotten up. How do you say in Spanish...shouldn't we wait for the sun?

I slipped on my *chopos*. Slippers were a must year-round on these icy cold floors. I tiptoed past Annalisa's bed and left her to dream away.

Grandpa and I ate our breakfast of bacon and fried eggs, homemade *tortillas*, and *atole*.

Atole is a hot cereal made of blue corn meal. It was a special breakfast treat I looked forward to eating whenever we visited Grandpa's house.

In the *casita* Grandpa began the weaving lesson. He was talking about *las canillas, el campo,* and *la labor.* I panicked! I didn't understand any of these words!

Then he pointed to the huge wooden box where the wool was kept.

I walked over and lifted the lid. I felt better when I smelled the familiar fragrance of wool. I imagined the colorful skeins and spools of wool were jewels in a treasure chest.

There were spools of turquoise blue, jet black, pearl white, ruby red, and emerald green. The skeins of reddish brown, rust, and grey made me think of the sandstone hills nearby.

Grandpa suggested I choose seven colors. One for the background, *el campo*, and the other six colors to create the border, *la zanefa*, and the design, *la labor*. Grandpa showed me how to wind the wool onto the spools, *las canillas*. He placed the spools into hand-carved shuttles, or *lanzaderas*.

Grandpa wanted me to begin on the smaller loom. This loom was used for weaving narrow rugs and small weavings called *congas*.

First he wove in a long, heavy string to make an even beginning. Then he pushed a shuttle of red wool across the warp and stepped down on one of the foot pedals. This moved the bottom warp to the top and the top warp to the bottom.

Grandpa then firmly banged the beater twice against the weft to tighten the wool in place. The weft is the wool that makes the design.

Grandpa stepped down so I could begin.

I stepped up to face the loom. I slid the shuttle between the strands of warp, stepped down on the left pedal, no on the right, no I was correct the first time! Next I reached for the beater to tighten the strands of weft together. I felt so clumsy! I peered over my shoulder at Grandpa, and he calmly nodded at me to continue. Then *el tejedor* turned toward his loom.

He began immediately. I heard his shuttle swish across the warp. Then—bam-bam—he pulled the beater twice, tightening the weft. The foot pedals clattered under Grandpa's feet.

Swish-bam-bam-clatter, swish-bam-bam-clatter...

At last I was weaving! My smaller loom was making the same sounds as his, swish-bam-bam-clatter...over and over! This was so easy!

Already I was planning the next *conga*!

Lunch didn't go by quickly enough. After helping Annalisa with the dishes, I asked her to join us in the *casita*.

Grandpa showed me how and when to change colors to create the unique Chimayó designs. I felt sure of myself! With Annalisa there, I wanted to show off a little.

Grandpa and I were making music. Swish-bam-bam-clatter, swish-bam-bam-clatter, swish-bam.

Suddenly I felt his eyes on me.

Uh-oh.

I looked up and asked, "*¿Qué*, Grandpa?"

What had I done?

Grandpa's fingers moved softly across the cloth. He slowly shook his head and asked, "*¿Porqué estás tan apurada?*"

"Grandpa wants to know why you are in such a hurry." said Annalisa.

"*Cuida las orillas.*"

"He says, 'watch the edges,'" she continued.

"*¿Qué no vas a usar el azul aquí en la labor?*"

I was embarrassed. My hands turned icy cold.

Annalisa moved closer to my loom and quietly said, "Grandpa wants to know if you're going to use blue in the design."

Even though he spoke in an understanding way, I felt like a *tonta*, stupid.

Annalisa went on translating for me. She said Grandpa wanted me to concentrate and go a little slower.

Grandpa returned to his weaving and Annalisa went back to the house. I looked at my *conga*. I slowly began undoing the weave.

My aunt had said, "All you have to do is listen

and learn the best you can." I knew that I wanted
to do my best. So I would take the whole thing
apart and start over again.

That evening Mom and Dad called.

Grandpa spoke with them first. "*Sí, sí, la Cristina está aprendiendo muy bien.*"

I didn't understand enough Spanish to keep up with the rest of their conversation, but before too long Grandpa called me to the phone.

"Hello *Jita*, how is everything?" my dad asked.

"Oh, we're doing fine, Dad."

"And how about the weaving?"

I was hoping he wouldn't ask me about weaving.

"It didn't go so well today. The edges were uneven and I left out one of the colors."

"What did you do?"

"I undid everything and started over."

"Well, I think you made the right decision because Grandpa says you're learning very well. *Oye*, don't be so hard on yourself."

That made me feel better!

The next morning Grandpa and I returned to our looms.

I worked at a much slower pace. Today I would do everything right. I placed the spools of wool, *las canillas*, on a table next to the loom in the order of colors that I planned to use. I didn't want to make the same mistake twice!

For many hours my Grandpa and I moved our shuttles back and forth in the familiar rhythm, swish-bam-bam-clatter, swish-bam-bam-clatter.

By the end of the day I had half of the weaving done. I felt I had made good progress.

The next day was Saturday. It was irrigation day for Grandpa. Annalisa and I asked if we could help.

The three of us watched as water flowed into each row of vegetables. Grandpa showed us how to clear the way with our hoes so that the water could run freely.

He always grew many vegetables. There were beans, chile, corn, cucumber plants, and *calabacita.*

Calabacita is a small pumpkin that my Grandpa used in one of my favorite dishes. He fried *calabacita*, fresh corn, green chile, and onions together. Then he'd sprinkle cheese over.

We snacked on tomatoes fresh off the vine. Oh, they were the best and the juiciest!

We asked Grandpa if we were going to irrigate the orchards, too.

He explained that other farmers needed to irrigate. It was necessary for people in the community to share the ditch water.

By early afternoon the three of us set our muddy shoes out to dry and cleaned ourselves up. I plopped myself down on the old sofa. Annalisa chuckled and said, "Don't get too comfortable. Grandpa has something planned for you! *Prima*, you are about to get a lesson in making whole wheat *tortillas*!"

Sure enough, Grandpa had washed his hands and was pulling a large bowl off the shelf. *"Cristina, venga 'ca, por favor*—come here, please," he called from the kitchen.

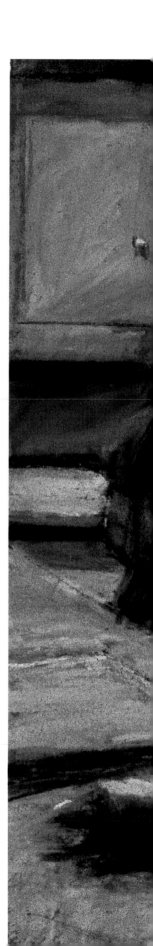

Annalisa giggled as the two of us redheads teamed up to make *tortillas*. Whole wheat flour, salt, and baking powder were mixed with *manteca de jamón*, which is bacon grease, and warm water. When all the ingredients were mixed together, Grandpa formed the *masa*, the dough, into a big ball. He covered the bowl with a cloth and set it aside for about twenty minutes.

Later Grandpa and Annalisa tore off pieces of the dough and rolled them into small balls, *bolitas*.

We laughed as I began flattening the *bolitas* with a homemade rolling pin called a *bolillo*. My *tortillas* did not come out round like they were supposed to. They came out in strange shapes, like the shapes of countries I saw on the maps at school.

Grandpa placed them one by one on the hot *comal*. He used this round iron griddle every day to make and heat *tortillas*.

Soon the smell of *tortillas* cooking filled the kitchen. It made all of us very hungry.

Sunday morning Annalisa, Grandpa, and I stepped out into the warm sunshine. We began our walk up the road toward El Buen Pastor Presbyterian Church. Without question, Sunday was church day and a day of rest for Grandpa.

After the service Annalisa and I were introduced to Grandpa's many friends who called him "Red." He got that nickname when he was young because of his red hair. Even now, when his hair was nearly white, he was still "*Tío* Red" or "*el* Red" to his old friends.

I met some relatives who sent their greetings to Ambrosio and Eva, my parents. Grandpa told everyone he was happy to have two of his grandchildren staying with him.

Grandpa and I were weaving the next morning when *Tía Elcia* beeped the car horn. She had come to pick up Annalisa to go to the grocery store. *Tía* came into the *casita* and headed straight for the light hanging above the loom. Switch, it went on!

"*¿Papá, porqué no prende la luz?*" She was asking why he didn't turn on the light.

Grandpa just kept on weaving and reminded his daughter to bring milk and butter from the store.

She looked at my weaving, hugged me, and turned to leave. With a smile she said, "He'll turn off the light after I've gone. He doesn't want to waste electricity."

Grandpa waited until *Tía Elcia* had driven away. He reached for the string and switched off the light. "*¿Porqué usar la luz cuando hay sol?*"

Why use the light when you have the sun?

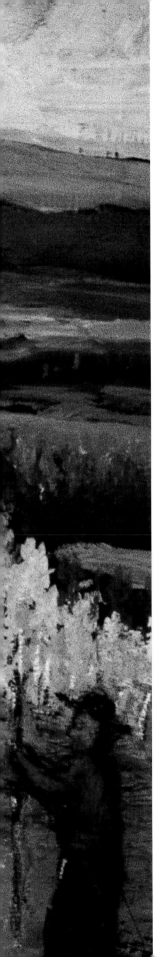

Now Grandpa and I were really alone.

In between the swish-bam-bam-clatters of our looms I heard a gruff humming sound. It didn't take me long to figure out Grandpa was singing.

I thought maybe he had forgotten that I was in the room because it was like he was singing to himself. After a while he began telling me *cuentos*, stories of when he was a young man. "*Yo viajé en el tren*," he told me. He traveled on the train through southern Colorado to work on ranches and on the railroad. He told me about his adventures herding sheep, *borregas*, in the high Rocky Mountains.

I didn't understand everything he said but enough to enjoy his *cuentos*. He was some storyteller!

I was nearly done with the *conga* by the time the sun moved toward the western sky. This was my last day to weave. I realized I didn't want it to end. Sadness fell over me.

The shuttle glided across the warp one last time. *El tejedor* picked up the scissors and began cutting the ends to release the cloth, *la tela*. I held my breath as he placed the cloth in my hands.

Then he walked away. Had I done a terrible job? Was he disappointed?

I wiped a tear from my eye as he came back into the room.

Wrapped over his arm was a weaving the size of mine. It was one that he had woven years ago. Grandpa folded my *conga* twice and put it on the table. It stood stiff, at attention. He did the same to the older *conga* and placed it next to mine. It fell softly like a piece of velvet. Grandpa smiled and said, "*Mira, así es como la quieres.*"

I looked up at him and looked back at the old conga. He was telling me that that was how I wanted mine to be.

I understood him. "*Sí Grandpa, yo entiendo,*" I whispered.

El tejedor told me not to make myself so sad. "*No te pongas tan triste.*" He added, "*Has tejido una buena conga. Pero se necesita práctica y paciencia.*"

I let out a sigh of relief as he spoke! I had woven a good *conga*. But he was right. I needed practice and patience.

Grandpa placed the older conga over my arm and said, "*La conguita vieja es para ti.*" The older *conga* was for me.

"*Muchisimas gracias*, Grandpa," I said.

I thought of Grandpa's father and all the
Ortega weavers before him. I saw how happy he
was to pass the family tradition on to me. I smiled
when I saw the twinkle *en los ojos del tejedor.*

GLOSSARY (GLOSARIO)

ESPAÑOL (SPANISH)	INGLES (ENGLISH)
(un) abrazo	a hug
(el) almuerzo	breakfast
aprendiendo (aprender)	learning (to learn)
apurada (apurar)	hurry
azul	blue
(un) besito	a little kiss
bolillo	homemade rolling pin
bolitas	small balls
(las) borregas	sheep

ESPAÑOL (SPANISH)	INGLES (ENGLISH)
buenas noches	good night
bueno	good
calabacita	small pumpkin
(el) campo	background color for the weaving
canillas	spools on which wool is wound
(la) casita	small house
Chimayó	small village in northern New Mexico
chopos (slang)	slippers
cómo	how
conga	a small version of the Chimayó blanket
cuando	when
cuentos	stories
cuida (cuidar)	watch (to watch, to pay attention to)
cuida las orillas	watch the edges (selvages)
ella	she
Ella está aprendiendo muy bién.	She is learning very well.
entender	to understand
¿entienden?	do you understand?
gracias	thank you
hacer	to do
Has tejido una buena conga, pero se necesita práctica y paciencia.	You have woven a good blanket, but you need to practice and to have patience.
hay	there is
(la) jita	little daughter
La conguita vieja es para ti.	The old blanket is for you.

ESPAÑOL (SPANISH)	INGLES (ENGLISH)
(la) labor	design woven into the blanket
(las) lanzaderas	hand-carved wooden shuttles
levántate (levantar)	get up (to get up)
los ojos del tejedor	the eyes of the weaver
(la) luz	the light
(la) manteca de jamón	bacon grease
(la) masa	dough
mi jita	my little daughter
Mira, así es como lo quieres.	Look, this is how you want it.
(el) mono (slang)	television set
muchísimas gracias	thank you very much
mucho	much
muy bien	very well
necesita (necesitar)	need
no, gracias	no, thank you
No te pongas tan triste.	Don't make yourself so sad.
¿Oh sí?	Oh yes ?(really?)
(los) ojos	eyes
(las) orillas	edges
para tí	for you
(la) paciencia	patience
pero	but, however
pongas (poner)	become
¿porque?	why?
¿Porqué estás tan apurada?	Why are you in such a hurry?
¿Porqué no prende la luz?	Why don't you turn the light on?
¿Porqué usar luz cuando hay sol?	Why use light when there is sun?
(la) practica	practice

ESPAÑOL (SPANISH)	INGLES (ENGLISH)
(la) prima	cousin (female)
¿Qué, Grandpa?	What, Grandpa?
¿Qué no vas a usar el azul aquí en la labor?	Aren't you going to use blue in the design?
quieres (querer)	you want (to want)
Sangre de Cristo	blood of Christ
(el) sol	sun
(una) sonrisa	a smile
(el) tejedor	weaver
tejido (tejer)	woven (to weave)
(la) tela	cloth
Tenemos mucho que hacer.	We have much to do.
tener	to have
Tía Elcia	Aunt Elsie
tonta	stupid (slang)
(las) tortillas	tortillas (round flatbread made from corn or wheat)
(el) tren	train
triste	sad
Venga'ca, por favor.	Come here, please.
viajó (viajar)	traveled
viejo, vieja	old
y	and
Ya está el almuerzo.	Breakfast is ready.
yo	I
Yo viajé en el tren.	I travelled on the train.
(la) zanefa	border

CRISTINA ORTEGA

Cristina Ortega is a descendant of Spanish Colonial settlers and granddaughter of El Tejedor—the weaver who is the subject of this book. With this and future books she hopes to introduce young readers to a unique Hispanic culture that is little known outside the Southwest. A writer and experienced elementary school teacher, Ortega resides in Albuquerque.

PATRICIO E. GARCÍA

1935–2005

Patricio García's luminous pastels evoke the landscape and spirit of the mountain villages of New Mexico. Illustrations from this book were exhibited in a one-man show at the Governor's Gallery in Santa Fe, New Mexico. Patricio was a native of northern New Mexico.